0033.8765.123456

This edition published by Kids Can Press in 2017

Text copyright © Ingrid Chabbert
Illustrations copyright © Guridi
First published in France in 2015 by © Éditions Frimousse
Translation rights arranged through the VeroK Agency, Barcelona, Spain

English translation © 2017 Kids Can Press

Kids Can Press gratefully acknowledges the financial support of the
Government of Ontario, through the Ontario Media Development Corporation.

Published in Canada and the U.S. by Kids Can Press Ltd.
25 Dockside Drive, Toronto, ON M5A 0B5

Kids Can Press is a Corus Entertainment Inc. company

www.kidscanpress.com

The artwork in this book was rendered in charcoal, gravure ink, gouac
pencil and digitally.
The text is set in Cochin LT Std.

English edition edited by Jennifer St

Printed and bound in Malaysia in 9/2016 by Tie

CM 17 0 9 8 7 6 5 4 3 2 1

Library and Archives Canada Cataloguing in   cation

Chabbert, Ingrid, 1978–
[Dernier arbre. English]
The last tree / written by Ingrid Chabbert ; illustrated by Raúl Nieto Guridi.

Translation of: Le dernier arbre.
ISBN 978-1-77138-728-6 (hardback)

I. Nieto Guridi, Raúl, 1970–, illustrator II. Title. III. Title: Dernier arbre. English.

PZ7.C349La 2017   j843´.92   C2016-902576-4

THE LAST TREE

Written by Ingrid Chabbert

Illustrated by Guridi

Kids Can Press

When I was a boy,
besides being small for my age,
I was enormously bored.

To entertain me,
my dad told stories about the world
when he was young.

His favorite thing was rolling around
in the grass with his best friend.

Cartwheels on Monday, leapfrog on
Wednesday and kite-flying on Sunday.

I had a best friend, too.

But not the grass to go with him.
Instead, we had roads, walls and
lots of other ugly things.

Actually, there was a bit of grass left.

You had to go a long way to get to it.
Sometimes I cycled there because it was faster.
But I couldn't roll around in it,
and I couldn't walk on it barefoot.

One day, I counted the blades of grass.
1, 2, 3, 4 … 13.

There were only thirteen left.
The week before, there'd been seventeen.

When I got home,
I lost myself in my books.
To see some green, some leaves …
some happiness.

The next day, Gus,
my best friend, came to find me.

"You have to see this,"
he told me in secret.

We jumped on our bikes
and I followed him.
I followed him for such
a long time my legs hurt.

"We're here!" he said, finally.

We got off our bikes, and I kept following him.
And there, behind a low, crumbling wall,
a small tree was hiding.

It must have been a very young tree.

"It's so beautiful!" I whispered.
"It's the first one I've seen."
"Do you think it's the last tree?"
"Probably."

We stayed a long time, looking at it
without moving, without speaking.

That night, I dreamt about it.
I imagined it tall. Huge, even.
And majestic.

But the next day when I saw the front page of the newspaper on the kitchen table, I quickly understood that it would never be huge.

The headline read

247-Floor Luxury Condo!
Construction to start this week.

And next to the headline, a photo of the broken-down wall hiding our little tree.

EXT

The Daily

no.203.078

bla bla bla bla bla bla bla
bla bla bla bla bla bla bla bla
bla bla bla bla bla bla
bla bla bla bla bla bla
bla bla bla bla bla
bla bla bla bla bla bla bla bla

bla bla bla bla bla bla bla bla
bla bla bla bla bla bla
bla bla bla bla bla bla bla
bla bla bla bla bla
bla bla bla bla bla bla bla
bla bla bla bla bla bla bla
bla bla bla bla bla bla bla
bla bla bla bla bla bla

bla bla bla bla bla bla bla
bla bla bla bla bla bla bla bla
bla bla bla bla bla bla
bla bla bla bla bla bla bla
bla bla bla bla bla bla bla
bla bla bla bla bla
bla bla bla bla bla bla
bla bla bla bla bla bla

RA!

veryday

Since 1802

247-Floor Luxury Condo! Construction to start this week.

bla bla bla bla bla bla
bla bla bla bla bla bla bla bla
bla bla bla bla bla bla bla bla
bla bla bla bla bla bla bla bla
bla bla bla bla bla bla
bla bla bla bla bla bla bla bla
bla bla bla bla bla bla bla
bla bla bla bla bla bla bla bla
bla bla bla bla bla bla bla
bla bla bla bla bla bla bla bla
bla bla bla bla bla bla

bla bla bla bla bla bla bla bla
bla bla bla bla bla bla
bla bla bla bla bla bla bla bla
bla bla bla bla bla bla bla
bla bla bla bla bla bla bla bla
bla bla bla bla bla bla bla bla
bla bla bla bla bla bla bla bla
bla bla bla bla bla bla bla bla
bla bla bla bla bla bla bla bla
bla bla bla bla bla bla bla bla

bla bla bla bla bla bla bla bla
bla bla bla bla bla bla bla bla
bla bla bla bla bla bla bla
bla bla bla bla bla bla bla
bla bla bla bla bla bla bla
bla bla bla bla bla bla bla bla
bla bla bla bla bla bla bla bla
bla bla bla bla bla bla bla
bla bla bla bla bla bla bla bla

bla bla bla bla bla bla bla bla
bla bla bla bla bla bla
bla bla bla bla bla bla bla bla
bla bla bla bla bla bla bla
bla bla bla bla bla bla bla bla
bla bla bla bla bla bla bla
bla bla bla bla bla bla bla bla
bla bla bla bla bla bla bla bla
bla bla bla bla bla bla bla bla
bla bla bla bla bla bla bla

la bla bla bla bla bla
a bla bla bla
la bla bla bla
a bla bla bla
bla bla bla bla bla bla
bla bla bla bla bla bla

bla bla bla bla bla bla bla bla
bla bla bla bla bla bla bla bla
bla bla bla bla bla bla bla bla
bla bla bla bla bla bla bla bla
bla bla bla bla bla bla bla
bla bla bla bla bla bla bla
bla bla bla bla bla bla bla
bla bla bla bla bla bla
bla bla bla bla bla bla
bla bla bla bla bla bla
bla bla bla bla bla

My parents looked on, surprised,
as I ran to the garage.
My bike was waiting.

Together, Gus and I rode as fast
as our legs and wheels could go.

The little tree was still there,
unaware of the threat
hanging over it.

I took a shovel from my backpack
and started to dig.
I had to get it out of there.

I gently took the tree, put it in my
backpack and got back on my bike.

We rode for so long, the early morning had turned into night when we stopped, exhausted.

This spot would be perfect.

We dug. And dug. And dug.
So it would do well in its new home.
I looked at it.
I looked at the stars
and asked them to watch over it.

It was the last tree.

Years later, I returned to see it.
I had grown.
The tree had, too.